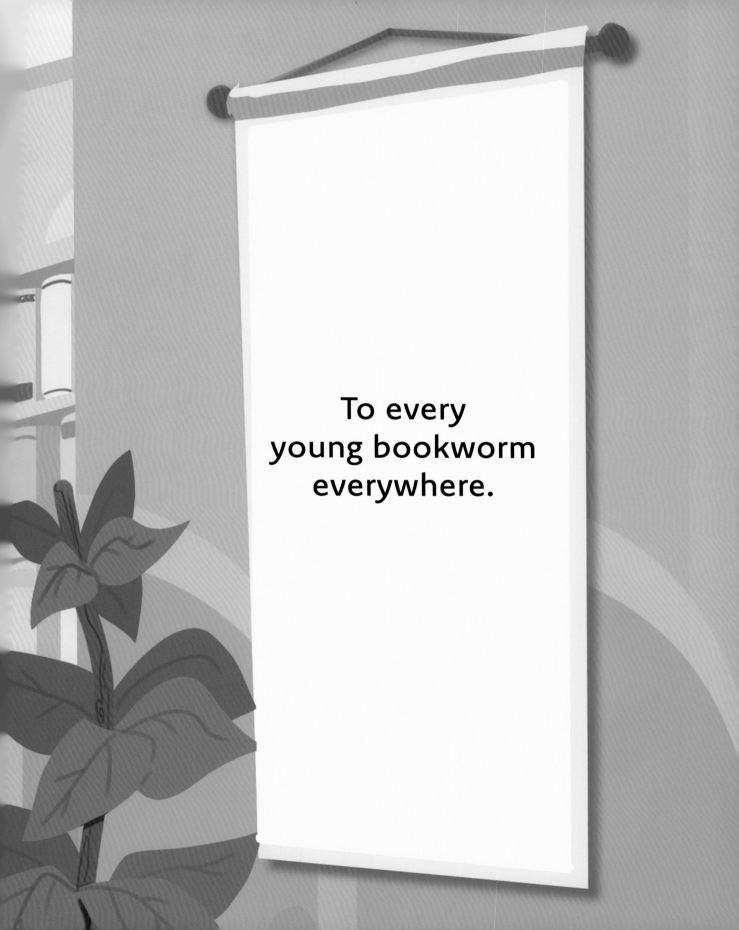

To every
young bookworm
everywhere.

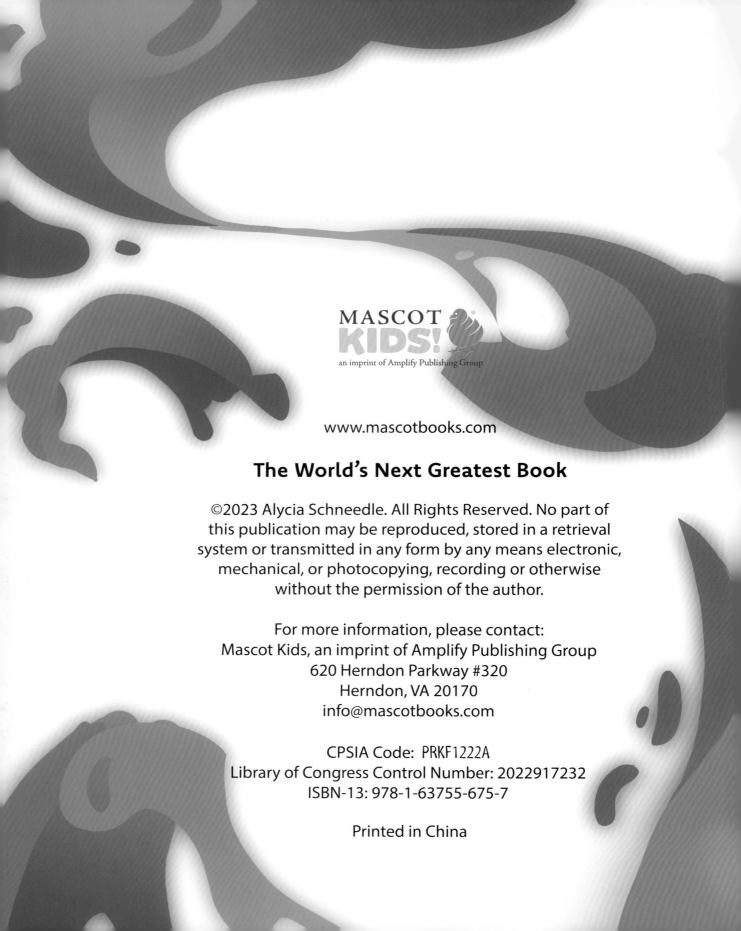

MASCOT KIDS!
an imprint of Amplify Publishing Group

www.mascotbooks.com

The World's Next Greatest Book

For more information, please contact:
Mascot Kids, an imprint of Amplify Publishing Group
620 Herndon Parkway #320
Herndon, VA 20170
info@mascotbooks.com

CPSIA Code: PRKF1222A
Library of Congress Control Number: 2022917232
ISBN-13: 978-1-63755-675-7

Printed in China

The World's Next Greatest
BOOK

Alycia Schneedle

Illustrated by
Juan Diaz

This is a story about a boy named Barry
at his most favorite place—the public library.
With its shelves and rows of stories stacked high,
and books about everything—it's an endless supply!

Barry loves reading . . . he doesn't find it hard.
He's the proud owner of his very own library card.

Enchantville
Public
Library
Card

Barry
Bookman

He's read so many stories, both fact and fiction.
He's been called a bookworm, an accurate description.

There's nothing better to Barry
than a good, long book. . .

that transports you to another
world, right from the hook.

One rainy morning at Barry's most favorite place,
he was reading a story about outer space.
When Barry was finished, he closed the cover
and returned to the children's section to select another.

He searched through the books on the five shelves stacked tal
and suddenly realized he'd read them all!

He searched high and low in every direction,
but he'd read everything in the children's book section.

Oh no, he thought. *This cannot be true.*
If I've read all the books, now what will I do?

He turned back to the shelves to look for more,
when he found one he was sure
hadn't been there before . . .

It was the very last book on the bottom right row, and as soon as he touched it, it started to glow.

The book had no title, just that strange glowing hue.
It simply said, "Author," followed by, "YOU."

How odd, Barry thought. *What does that mean?*
He turned the front cover of the book that glowed green,

ut when he flipped through the pages, his heart suddenly sank.
his book had no story . . . all the pages were blank!

He looked back at the spot where the strange book had been and that's when he spotted a bright green glowing pen.

He stared at the word, "Author,"
then at the word, "YOU."
That's when it struck him.
He knew just what to do.

He took both glowing objects and sat down at a table
to write his own story, *The World's Next Greatest Fable.*
He sat and he wrote and wrote then wrote some more.
He wrote more than he'd ever written before,
about a magical kingdom a hero defends
with the help of a group of courageous young friends
against a huge monster while on a quest for treasure.
It was fun and scary in equal parts measure.

As soon as he wrote the final words, "The End,"
the strange book stopped glowing, and so did the green pen
The World's Next Greatest Fable, the title now read,
and where it had said, "Author," was his name instead.

The World's Next Greatest Fable

By
Barry Bookman

Barry picked up the book and brought it back to its shelf,
armed with this new knowledge and proud of himself.
When he runs out of books, Barry now knew,
the world's next greatest book . . .
can be written by **YOU.**

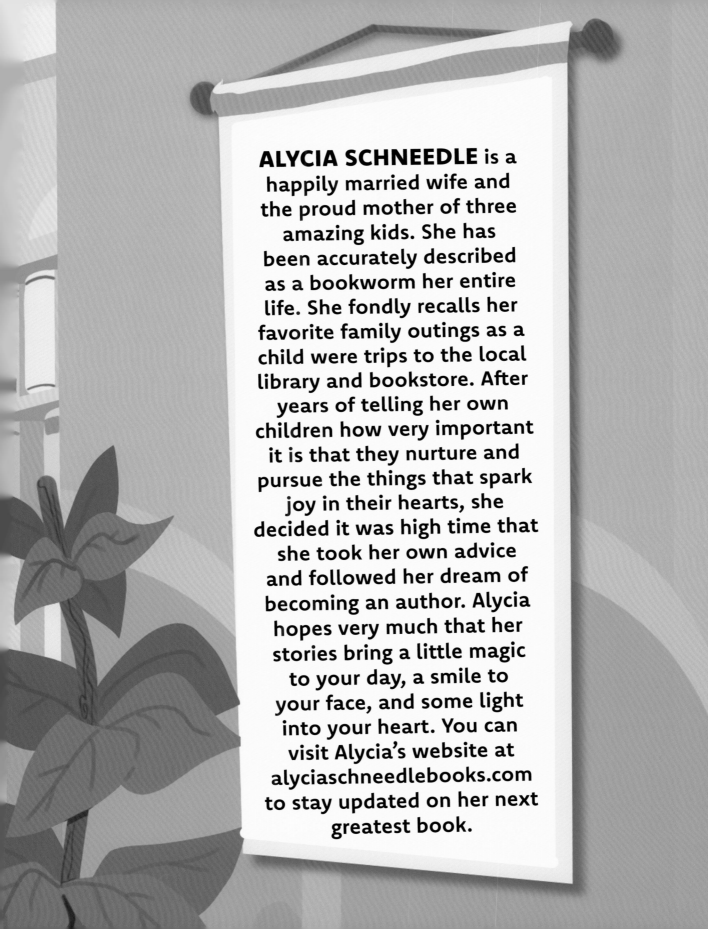

ALYCIA SCHNEEDLE is a happily married wife and the proud mother of three amazing kids. She has been accurately described as a bookworm her entire life. She fondly recalls her favorite family outings as a child were trips to the local library and bookstore. After years of telling her own children how very important it is that they nurture and pursue the things that spark joy in their hearts, she decided it was high time that she took her own advice and followed her dream of becoming an author. Alycia hopes very much that her stories bring a little magic to your day, a smile to your face, and some light into your heart. You can visit Alycia's website at alyciaschneedlebooks.com to stay updated on her next greatest book.